The Arizona Kid

Elena E Smith

Published by Books For Boomers, 2024.

THE ARIZONA KID

First edition. July 7, 2024.

Copyright © 2024 Elena E Smith.

ISBN: 979-8227037688

Written by Elena E Smith.

Table of Contents

The Arizona Kid 1

O Holy Night 2

Just Ask 9

The Gift..20

Orange Moe..25

"Who Is Itt?" 38

The Overnight...54

Acknowledgments:...67

Also by this author: 68

To Supai Memories

Cover Art by Cheryl Ryan https://cherylryan.com/

The following two stories have been previously published on-line:

O Holy Night (Kings River Life Magazine, Dec. 2022)
Who Is Itt? (Kings River Life Magazine, Oct. 2021)

O Holy Night

5th Grade, December 1965

I've heard some people think growing up on a ranch is fun. At times, it could be. But it definitely had its downside -—getting up at four a.m. to feed the cows or walking to school with dried grey muck on your shoes. Boys don't care about that stuff, but when you're a girl, it can be embarrassing to show up at school smelling like a barnyard. And back when I grew up, we didn't have a mall nearby where we could buy "body splash" to cover it up with.

I wasn't a good student or a bad student. I was the kind of kid nobody noticed much, with medium-length plain brown hair, big eyes and freckles. But there were a few things I could do really well. I could sing, I could dance, and I could do gymnastics. And whenever my parents and my brothers left me home alone, I transformed our small living room into a stage. I held a flashlight upside down and sang into the big end like it was a microphone, prancing over and around the furniture. I played this game for hours, and my life changed for the better when I met Beth because she loved to sing, too, and we staged duets, concerts and sing-offs in my empty living room on a regular basis. Beth was much prettier than me, with naturally blond hair, and she was taller and not as skinny as I was. She had better clothes, too, and more confidence. But when we sang together in my living room, with the lights turned down for atmosphere, we were equal, and sometimes I was even a little better than she was when a lower voice range was required.

Fall kicked in with a vengeance and the Arizona temperature dropped into the forties with a dry wind that found all the loose spots in our cable knit sweaters as we stood in line for the annual Christmas Pageant auditions. Every year, our school produced a play with costumes, a band concert and other entertainment, including the chance to be the soloist on O Holy Night. The day of try-outs, Beth and I waited with fifty other kids outside the school cafeteria, which also doubled as the auditorium, our hands pulled into our sleeves to preserve what little warmth we had.

A red-haired boy bumped by me and mumbled, "Smelly Nellie the Cattle Queen," in my ear, but I ignored him. I'd learned a long time ago that the kids who called names were often called a lot of names, themselves. Let me just say that red hair wasn't too popular at my school. A lot less popular than living on a ranch. But I had another reason for ignoring him, too -—my brothers, Jim and Curt. Once the redhead found out about them, he would forget about my dreaded nickname. And if he didn't forget soon enough, my brothers would help him do it. Weeks later, the class bully would see that "Smelly Nellie" became "Sweet Nellie" when Momma sent a batch of fresh-baked fudge nut brownies to the pageant for everyone to enjoy.

On the day of the pageant, I waited patiently in line for the janitor in grey coveralls to open the auditorium, as I clutched a frosty pie tin with a paper napkin covering the no-longer-warm sweet treats. Inside the auditorium, it was a zoo. Parents, kids with musical instruments and kids without musical instruments shed coats hats umbrellas purses on every available chair as Mr. Herndon, the band teacher, and Mrs. Zwick, the music teacher, yelled as loud as they could for us to put our personal belongings backstage, even though backstage was not much more than a narrow corridor behind the scrim curtain. I blended in with the milling mass that hustled up the six steps on one side of the stage, and was thrilled to see that the normally dusty, navy-colored scrim curtain had been painted with glittery white paint which transformed it into a jewel-like silhouette of Jerusalem, the Holy City. I wanted to enjoy it longer, but someone's elbow in my back pressed me to continue on behind the scrim where several long conference tables had been set up, and my fudge nut brownies soon joined the cookies, candy canes and fruit punch.

As I found a spot for my comfortable but tattered tan corduroy coat, I noticed the highly polished wood plank floor, amazed that the janitor had been able to remove the scuff marks from black patent leather shoes that had built up during weekly band rehearsals. With a pang, I remembered the auditions for the Christmas Pageant four weeks ago. I sang my heart out on O Holy Night, but it was no use. A low alto like me could not hit the A-above-high-C without a slight screech in my voice. And though I had practiced for weeks to adjust the screech to what I hoped was a less noticeable squeak, Mrs. Zwick smiled and said only, "Good work, Nellie. Next? Beth?"

Beth, of course, was chosen to sing O Holy Night. As a strong second soprano with a wide range, she glided easily over the notes that had taken me hours of practice to reach. I wasn't jealous. You see, Beth was my best friend. But I had hoped that practicing would make it possible to have the opportunity to be the soloist this year.

The cacophony of instruments tuning up, singing and laughing forced me to stop dwelling on my disappointment. The Pageant would last several hours, and each of us had something to prepare for, even if it was just to change into our shimmery dresses to be part of the back-up chorus.

I looked across the room and saw Beth at the refreshment table -—her blonde hair perfectly curled and glossy from hair spray. She had not changed into her sparkling white soloist dress, yet, and was still wearing blue jeans and a red plaid hunting shirt. I watched her rummage through the sweets, popping treats into her mouth, including one of Momma's fudge nut brownies. And that's when the problem started. Because, even though I knew that Beth was highly allergic to walnuts, it was the furthest thing from my mind at the moment. Mrs. Zwick began herding us to the dressing room and in one jostling noisy bunch, we moved away from the refreshment tables that would soon be placed elsewhere in preparation for the show.

It was about twenty minutes later -—as we girls seemed to be half in and half out of our costumes -—when someone screamed, "Beth, what's wrong with your face?"

We all turned to look, and sure enough, Beth's face had swollen like a balloon filled with water. She struggled for breath as it grew redder.

"Teacher!" someone cried out.

And, let me tell you, I wanted to crawl into a gopher hole and hide when I realized what had happened. Beth was having an allergic reaction to Momma's fudge nut brownies. She was going into anaphylactic shock. I knew about this because she'd explained it to me before, but I'd never seen it happen, and I realized that I had actually seen her pick up the fudge nut brownie -—and I hadn't said a word to stop her.

"Nellie!" Mrs. Zwick grabbed my arm at the same time the ambulance came wailing up to the back door of the auditorium. "Put on the white dress."

I just stared at her. "I can't—-"

"Do it. Now!"

"But, Mrs. Zwick," I stammered. "I know I'm supposed to be the understudy, but I can't hit the highest note."

"We'll transpose the key, if we have to," she said calmly. "You don't have to go on for an hour. You know the words, don't you?"

I nodded dumbly, wondering what "transpose the key" meant.

I couldn't tell you whether the hour went by too slowly or too quickly. Even though O Holy Night was my favorite of all songs, I dreaded the idea of singing a solo in front of the entire community and hitting the squeaky note near the finish. So, I cracked my knuckles. I paced. I practiced slow breathing and counting to ten, but I was a nervous wreck. Somewhere in my heart, I knew that I had seen Beth pick up that fudge nut brownie and I'd done nothing to stop her. Did I do it on purpose, so I could get the solo away from her?

Nearby, Mrs. Zwick and Mr. Herndon were talking in a loud whisper as the Hand Bell Choir performed on stage. She was an upbeat middle-aged pear-shaped woman who always dressed conservatively and had a smile for everyone. He was slightly older, thin and athletic with hair as short as teddy-bear fur and dry, reddish skin.

"But we can't," Mr. Herndon hissed. "You can re-key a song if you're using piano and vocals, but it's a different thing when you have a small orchestra. You can't just transpose the key so easily with all those instruments involved."

"It can't be that difficult—-," Mrs. Zwick protested.

"But it is. Not all instruments can play in all keys. Besides, these are kids. It was hard enough for them to learn their parts to begin with. We can't just change it on them at the last minute. They'll never be able to do it!"

A big knot of dread built in my stomach. Then, Mrs. Zwick saw me watching them. She came over to me, fiddled with my hair and adjusted the big shiny bow at the back of the soloist's dress.

"Nellie, why don't you sit down for a few minutes, over there," she said, and put her arm around my shoulders, leading me to a chair.

I looked out onto the stage from the sidelines. I kept seeing a cartoon character in my head running around in circles crying, "Woe is me!" I was responsible for single-handedly ruining the Christmas Pageant. First, I hadn't warned Beth about the fudge nut brownies, and now I was going to sing a song that was meant for her because of a high note I couldn't reach.

I sat down on the cold folding metal chair as the Hand Bell Choir left the stage and the pastor from the local Lutheran church walked briskly onto the platform with a serious look on his face. In his left hand, he carried a Bible that must have weighed ten pounds, and with his right hand he adjusted the height of a nearby black metal sheet music stand. He flopped the gold-leafed Bible onto the stand and it appeared to magically open to the exact page he planned to preach from.

I didn't have to listen because I already knew what he was going to say. "The Word of the Lord, from Matthew 1:21." He was going to tell the story of the birth of Jesus, just like every pastor did this time of year. "And she shall bring forth a son, and thou shalt call his name Jesus for he shall save his people from their sins," he intoned from his New King James Version.

As he continued, I couldn't help reflecting on my own sins of that day, and sank into a deeper level of misery as I realized that wrecking O Holy Night was going to be my punishment. But then the preacher's calm voice and encouraging words began to show me that I would get through it, even if I squealed on the high A. It wouldn't be easy, but by the time February came, everybody would be so busy talking about which boys would ask them to dance on Valentine's Day that my failure would be long forgotten. I felt myself sitting up a little taller in my chair as the thick red velvet curtain framing the front of the stage closed, removing the audience from view and turning the stage and backstage area into its own private navy and silver-white world. O Holy Night would be performed next, following the fifteen-minute break. I swallowed hard as the band members began to quietly move their chairs into a semi-circle in front of the scrim curtain where the Holy City shimmered under the Klieg lights.

"Beth!" someone cried out.

I looked up to see that Beth had entered the backstage area. Her face was still puffy after a hasty treatment of benadryl and adrenaline. I stood up quickly, worried that she would be furious with me for putting on the white soloist dress. In the background, I could hear Mrs. Zwick saying, "There isn't time to change."

"Then what do you suggest we do?" Beth's mother was asking in a strident voice.

I wanted to run, but as Beth's best friend, I knew that was the last thing I should do. So, I forced myself to get up off the chair and walk toward Beth and her mother, who looked at me, smiled, and said, "Hello, dear."

"You look nice," Beth agreed.

"But -—"

"We'll just have to put something over her face," Mrs. Zwick said, and she was right. The aftermath of Beth's asthma attack was going to draw far more attention than her beautiful voice would.

"I have an idea," Mrs. Zwick announced. "Nellie, you can dance, can't you?"

"Dance?" I echoed.

"You know, move around, like this?" She imitated some very basic ballet moves we had all practiced in gym class, but I couldn't imagine why she was asking me this.

I nodded.

"Then, we'll put Beth behind the scrim curtain. We'll light her from behind, which will make her look like an angel. She will sing the solo, and you, Nellie, will be at the front of the stage, moving in time to the music."

And that was how we performed O Holy Night at the Christmas Pageant that year. The reporter from the local paper really liked it, and only a few of us knew why the show had been changed from the way it was done before. I walked away that day with a special Christmas glow. I had a best friend who loved me, and who forgave me even when I didn't deserve it.

Just Ask

5th Grade, April 1966

"What's that?" Terry asked.

We were playing marbles in the soft dirt beside the donkey's corral -—Curt, Little Miguel and me -—and Terry had just ridden up on his bike, followed by his red-haired neighbor, Bobby. We'd drawn a circle in the dirt, and we'd each put in ten marbles, making an assortment of clearies, bumblebees, grasshoppers, swirlies, cat's eyes and a solid yellow boulder. I loved to look at the beautiful colors and patterns and didn't really like to play because when one of mine got knocked out of the circle the winner kept it, and I didn't like parting with any of my favorites. I put in as many cat's eyes as possible, because they were common and easy to replace. Some guys didn't care what kind of marbles they won, as long as there were lots of them in their marble bag, but it was different for me. I collected unique ones, and -—I didn't admit this to anyone, not even Curt or Terry -—all my pretty marbles had names.

Terry and Bobby dropped their bikes against the side of the donkey's pipe corral and it resounded like a gong. The donkey jumped sideways, rolled her eyes, and looked at the bikes suspiciously as the boys approached us to see the unusual marble my younger brother Curt was using against Little Miguel and me. Curt pinched a steelie in one of his chubby freckled hands. It was as small as a peewee but made of shiny metal. The heavier weight made it possible to knock a lot of marbles out of the circle and keep his turn going. During the twenty minutes we'd been playing, he'd added seven marbles to his pouch and it was still his turn.

"Where'd ya get that?" Terry wanted to know. It was the first time any of us had seen a steelie.

"Steve's dad brought it home from his workplace. He said it might be a ball bearing or something. As soon as I saw it, I wanted to win it, and I did," Curt said. His round blue eyes danced under his light brown hair. "I used my lucky boulder to win it off him."

Terry and Bobby mumbled admiringly, but I looked at Little Miguel, who'd just lost five of his ten marbles. I'd always thought Little Miguel was a cute six-year-old with his thick black hair in a bowl cut, and eyes so dark they were almost black. He was the son of our ranch hand, Miguel Perez. Their family lived in a small house at the edge of our fields. It was the house the original settlers lived in, nestled against a line of tall cottonwood trees planted by our great-grandparents as a windbreak. It was a two-room house made of wood, which was so old it had turned gray. Inside, there was a kitchen, where the family ate and where Little Miguel and the kids slept on the floor at night. The other room contained a sofa where his parents slept with the new baby.

"You get a pretty good hit with that," Bobby said.

"Yeah, if you have a good aim," Terry sneered sarcastically. "Show us what you can do."

Curt continued to play, cleaning out the circle, marble by marble. He even won my blue and white half-'n-half that I'd named Cadet after a color in my Crayola box. As my little brother slipped Cadet into a green striped marble bag made from an old sock, our eyes met and the twinkle I saw told me that he would give me a chance to win her back. Curt was the most generous one in our family.

"Wanna ride bikes?" Terry and Bobby asked me. "We're going over to the canal to see how high the water is, today."

It was almost 4:00, time for Wallace & Ladmo on TV. It was hot and dry, and if I went inside, there would be cold lemonade and probably some fresh pie or cookies.

"No, thanks," I said. "You guys have fun."

Terry gave Bobby a friendly shove. "Race ya!" and they ran to their Sting Rays.

They mounted quickly, like two cowboys chasing after lost dogies, and disappeared in a small dust devil.

Little Miguel looked at the almost-empty circle that held only two of his remaining marbles. Unless Curt lost his turn, Miguel would never get a chance to win any of them back. Curt took aim again, and quickly captured Miguel's last two. As Poppa's old blue truck pulled up in the drive, Curt decided he was ready to quit. Scooping the mass of marbles into his bag, he got up to go inside. Little Miguel grasped the small burlap flour sack he'd adopted as his marble bag. It was now completely empty. His lower lip trembled. I felt sorry for him, but I didn't know what to say, so I got to my feet after gathering my remaining marbles and said, "Better luck next time."

As I walked toward the house, I heard him whimpering.

* * *

At supper that night, everyone talked about how the Giants were doing at spring training camp while we finished our hamburgers and potato chips. Whenever we were on vacation from school, Momma would give us a break from meat-potato-vegetable dinners and make the stuff we really liked -—hamburgers, pizza or Sloppy Joes.

After the meal, when Momma began clearing the table, Poppa read from the Bible: "'A bruised reed, He will not break.' What do you think that means?"

I looked at the boys, hoping one of them would know the answer, but they each stared into their bowls of Neapolitan ice cream and spooned the melted part over the frozen top.

"What's a reed?" Curt finally asked.

"Well," Poppa said, "a reed is like a blade of grass, only taller and stiffer, and not as skinny. And, although they are sturdier than the kind of grass we have, they can still be beaten down by bad weather or when a person or animal steps on them. In time, it can grow tall again, unless someone snaps it off, breaking it. What do you think the Word is telling us tonight, about how to treat others?" He looked at my oldest brother, Jim, who was self-consciously pushing his dark bangs out of his eyes.

"Don't kick a guy when he's down?"

"Exactly," Poppa said proudly. Then, he picked up his spoon and began eating his dessert, as though that settled it and we all knew what he meant.

* * *

After dinner, the boys and I sat outside on the cement back porch steps. The sun was still up, and those steps were as warm as Momma's oven after Sunday dinner. We were sitting in age order -—Curt, the youngest, on one end with his round face, blond hair and blue eyes; me, brown hair and freckles, in the middle; and black-haired blue-eyed Jim, at the other end. He was already in his first year of high school.

"Did one of you guys kick somebody, today?" Jim asked.

"No!" we both cried.

"Then why did Poppa—-?"

"I have no idea," Curt said. "You know how he is with his scriptures; they don't always make sense, but he thinks they're important because they're in the Bible."

"Well, I agree that sometimes they don't make sense on the surface," Jim said carefully, "but I've found that when Poppa gives us a verse, he does it for a reason."

Curt and I looked at each other accusingly because we were both thinking the same thing: 'Did you kick somebody today?'

"You know," Jim continued, "in my English class our teacher told us how something could have a figurative meaning instead of a literal one."

"What does afigurative mean?" I asked.

"Figurative means it represents something, like a symbol. For example, Momma and Poppa both wear wedding rings, right? The rings are a symbol of their marriage. But if they took their rings off, or lost them, they'd still be married, right?"

"Of course!" Curt said, as if this was the dumbest question in the world.

"So, when Poppa talked about 'not kicking a man when he's down,' it doesn't mean literally kicking somebody, does it?"

Curt was baffled. "Well, I didn't kick anybody, so what does it mean?"

"Well, if a person is down, if they don't have very much, then it can hurt them when things don't go their way. Like, let's say a kid has three baseball gloves, and he loses one. Well, he can still play the game, because he has two more. But if a kid only has one baseball glove, and it gets ruined, he has nothing to catch the ball with, right?"

I was beginning to get an idea of what he meant, but Curt didn't get it, yet.

"You mean Little Miguel, don't you?" I asked.

"Right," Jim said.

Curt was quiet and started picking up some sharp-edged rocks near his feet and jiggling them back and forth in his hands.

I went on, "Because his family is poor, and he only had ten marbles to play with. But today, Curt won them all with his new steelie, so now Miguel can't play marbles anymore."

"Right," Jim said.

Curt picked up a stick and drew a circle in the dust, then scratched it out and threw the stick onto some grass.

He sighed. "I didn't think of it that way."

"Of course not," Jim said kindly.

"So, I guess I better figure out how to make it right." He picked up another stick, made a circle, and scratched it out.

"I know!" he beamed. "I'll let him use my steelie to win all his marbles back."

* * *

Curt's intentions were good, but things didn't go as planned. The next afternoon, just about the time I was supposed to run over to Little Miguel's house to fetch him, Terry and Bobby rode up on bikes, slamming them to the ground.

"I'm ready," Terry announced, strutting toward Curt and me, with Bobby close behind him.

We weren't sure what he was ready for.

"Bobby and I saw how you played yesterday with that silver peewee," Terry said, "and I don't think you can play any better than you normally do."

Curt was surprised by the challenge, but like most boys two years younger than Terry --—and me --—he was pleased to get the attention.

"So, you wanna play me, then?" Curt asked.

"Yeah," Terry said, dropping down to his knees, where his tan chinos immediately absorbed a layer of dusty earth. He reached for the belt loop at his waist where a brown and black leather sack was tied, and poured out marbles of various colors and sizes.

"We play ten each," Terry said.

Curt reached into his green-and-white sock-bag and counted out the ones he'd use.

Terry looked at Bobby, squatting behind him, and Bobby tossed his head as if to say, "Go get 'em." I was nervous, because I knew Terry better than anybody else did, and I knew he didn't like to lose. He thought he was the best at everything; that's why there were some games I wouldn't play with him.

Little Miguel appeared behind the boys and watched the game.

"You go first," Curt said politely.

Terry pulled out his best shooter, an oxblood swirlie, and carefully took aim. He shot several cat's eyes out of the circle, capturing the ones closest to the edges, going for the easy wins first. But once he had all of those, he shot into the ring again and nothing happened, stranding his best shooter. Now, Curt took aim with the steelie, and as Little Miguel's eyes grew wide, the force of the steelie knocked the oxblood swirlie out of the ring.

Terry jumped to his feet. "That's not fair! You cheated!"

Bobby jumped up right behind him, fists on his hips.

Curt was surprised by the reaction. "What did I do that was cheating?" he asked.

Bobby whispered something that only Terry could hear, and Terry spoke. "That's not a real marble, it's a ball bearing. Give me my oxxie back, and I'll forget about the whole thing."

Bobby whispered something else, and Terry spoke again. "Anyway that steelie is heavier than all the other marbles, and that's why you can win with it. It's not because you play so great."

Curt was still on his haunches, unsure how to respond, and before he got more time to think about it, Terry reached over and shoved his shoulder, tipping him backward. Curt wasn't hurt, but he couldn't let Terry push him around. He sprang to his feet and shoved him back, and the only reason Terry budged was from surprise. Terry was much bigger than Curt and could have whooped him easily.

"Take it back!" Curt said, leaning forward.

Terry shoved him again, and Curt toppled over. I could see this wasn't going to end well.

"Stop it, you guys!" I said in my fiercest shriek, hoping Momma would hear me and come out of the house.

Curt's pant leg was torn at the knee, but he got up again. I grabbed at his arm. "Don't, Curt, he's bigger than you—-"

"Nobody calls me a cheater in my own back yard," Curt huffed, a bright flush covering his cheeks.

Terry shoved him hard, and he went flying, landing on his butt. Bobby whispered something else, and I turned to run toward the house. Then the back screen door flew open with a bang, and Momma stood there with a rolling pin in her hand, interrupted during her afternoon baking. Suddenly, Terry and Bobby thought of somewhere else they'd rather be and ran for their bikes. Curt was the maddest I'd ever seen him.

As Terry and Bobby raced away, Terry looked over his shoulder at me and yelled, "You're not my friend anymore!"

"What's going on?" Momma called out.

"Nothin," Curt said hotly.

"Are you alright?" she asked.

"I'm fine," he said, getting to his feet and brushing off his pants.

Little Miguel had disappeared, and it was just the two of us. Momma surveyed the damage from her place on the stoop, figured it was under control, and let the screen door slam shut as she returned to her kitchen.

Curt looked at the ground, and suddenly his eyes narrowed. "That rat fink! He kyped my steelie!"

* * *

That night, we had a bar-b-que. Poppa and Momma always gave one when we sold a cow. The Perez family joined us at the two picnic tables and a spool table in our back yard. Despite the tense afternoon, the mood at dinner was festive, with Little Miguel and Curt running around and playing tag together as if there had never been a steelie. The only unpleasantness for me was during the cooking, when Terry rode by on his bike with his fishing pole on his way to Hole-In-The-Rock Park. For the last year, he'd jingle his bike bell every time he passed our farm, but this time he didn't. He did look over at me, but it was only to make an ugly face.

After we'd eaten everything we possibly could, and Mrs. Perez helped Momma clear the tables, we settled down by the pit where Poppa built a fire on special occasions. Momma produced a sack of marshmallows, and the boys ran to gather sticks. As we seared our treats over the flame, and the sun sank lower in the sky, Poppa brought out his Bible. He beckoned to Little Miguel, who climbed up onto the picnic table and snuggled against Poppa's side, then Poppa opened the Word and began to read:

"'Ask, and it shall be given you... For what man is there of you whom if his son ask bread will he give him a stone? Or, if he ask a fish, will he give him a serpent?' Nellie, what do you think this passage is about?"

I hated it when Poppa called on me during a scripture study, because I was never sure of the answer. I glanced around the circle, watching Little Miguel's fidgeting hands in his front pants' pockets, and Jim's half-closed eyes fixed on the sunset as he munched the end of his marshmallow stick. Jim liked to appear as though he wasn't paying attention but whenever there was a question, he always seemed to know the answer.

"Jim?" Poppa prodded.

Without looking away from the red hills against the blue and orange horizon, he said, "If there is something we need, all we have to do is ask?"

"Very good. And what about the way we treat each other, like the father and son the Bible describes? If we are all friends who care for one another, is there anyone here who wouldn't give what another asked for, if he was able?"

I didn't get the meaning. I looked around at all the faces, and saw Curt playing with his stick, Jim scratching the back of his head, Little Miguel still fiddling around.

"If there was another hamburger on the grill, do you think Momma would give it to me, or do you think she would give me a snake?"

We laughed at the absurdity. I looked over at Curt, who was drawing circles in the dirt, which meant he was listening closely to Poppa and thinking. Then, Poppa looked right at him. "Son, do you have something you want to say?"

Curt stood up and faced Little Miguel. "I'm sorry I won all your marbles away," he said. "I came up with a plan -—that I was gonna let you use my steelie to win 'em back -—but then Terry stole it from me. You can still win 'em all back from me; it just won't be with the steelie."

Little Miguel looked at him, his face bright with hope, then looked down but didn't say a word. A long silence fell on the group. We'd all been well-fed after a hot day and were getting sleepy. Poppa put his arm around Little Miguel, and I saw him whisper something encouraging.

An hour later, as we finished cleaning pots and pans in the kitchen, Poppa called Curt and me aside. There was a certain look Poppa would get that said, "I know something you don't know," but it was always a good thing.

"Curt, Nellie, why don't you go out to the pit and make sure the fire's been watered down enough?"

Curt and I looked at each other. What did "that look" have to do with a routine chore? We opened the back screen door and stepped onto the cement stoop, where we saw a wadded up washcloth, and lying on top of it was Curt's steelie. We wondered how Poppa knew it would be there.

"He must have seen Terry put it back," Curt said, still peeved about the episode.

"Just be glad," I said. I wanted my friendship with Terry to go back to normal.

Inside the house, Poppa was sitting in the living room on his recliner, and Momma sat on a nearby chair. Curt and I intended to go to our rooms, but Poppa beckoned.

"Is the fire completely out?" he asked.

"Yes."

"Find anything?"

We walked into the room.

"I got my steelie back," Curt said. "I guess that Terry—-"

"What makes you think it was Terry?" Poppa asked.

"Who else could it be? He was the one who got sore."

"The only one -—?"

"Well, besides Little Miguel," I said.

Then, it hit me. Little Miguel playing with something in his pocket all night; his low-key response when Curt told him he would let him win his marbles back...

"Sit down," Poppa said. "A lot of people can get hurt when there is a false accusation. Stealing is never the right solution to a problem, but sometimes a very young child doesn't realize their mistake until later. So, it's best to just forgive and forget if the problem has been solved. But you still have a problem, Curt."

"I do?"

"You have unfairly accused Terry."

Curt looked at the multicolor oval hook rug on our living room floor.

"I think you know what you need to do."

And, he did. He apologized to Terry the next day; he allowed Little Miguel to win all his marbles back using the steelie; and he put the steelie in the top drawer of his dresser, a prized possession that he would bring out only when asked.

The Gift

The screen door banged. Terry was the only guy I knew who walked into our house without knocking. It was late in the afternoon on Thanksgiving Day, and my parents were taking a nap. I was in the family room watching something stupid on TV and got up to meet him in the kitchen, where he'd stopped to scan the leftovers that were still on the counter. He reached for a slice of cherry pie.

"Eat it at your own risk," I cautioned.

He stopped. "Why?"

"Gramma brought that, and, you know..." He waited for me to continue. "Well, she's starting to lose her memory. Her pie used to be the best, but she put in salt instead of sugar, this time. Momma calls it her 'recipe for disaster.'"

"Ew, ick!" He drew back. "What else have you got?"

The bedroom door opened, and Momma emerged in her checkered house dress. "Terry, can I get you some cookies and milk?"

"Yes, please!"

Soon, we were seated on the davenport in the family room, scuffing our shoes on the rag rug. Terry eyed our robust Christmas tree as he gobbled his snack.

"What are you getting?" he asked with a mouth full of food.

I shrugged.

"I'm getting an album by Paul Revere and the Raiders," he bragged.

"Don't say that in front of Poppa; he'll think you're talking about a history book. Wait a minute. How do you know that?"

He smirked.

"Oh, I get it! The package. There's no way to disguise the shape of a record album." I looked wistfully at our tree, where I didn't see any thin square presents with my name on them.

"How do you know it's Paul Revere, and not some bubble gum group?" I teased.

"How do you think, knucklehead?" He slurped the last of his milk. "Don't you open your presents ahead of time?"

"Well, no! That would be like... like cheating!"

"Oh, come on, Nellie! Don't you wanna know what people got you?"

I'd never thought of it before. I was used to waiting for Christmas morning when our family made a big deal out of opening presents together. Terry jumped off the sofa and raced to the tree, his long brown bangs flopping against his forehead. He rummaged through the wrapped presents, fishing out a small square box.

He shook the package and looked at me. "What do you think it is?"

"Well—-"

"Don't you wanna know?" He tore the edge of the paper.

"Terry!"

Before I could stop him, he ripped the edge off.

"A Timex watch!" he announced.

"Terry!" I tackled him to the floor and we rolled around as I socked his arm, hoping I left a bruise.

He handed me the box in its crumpled wrapping. "Just tape it back up. No one will know."

"The person who wrapped it will know."

He thought I might start to cry, but I held it back. He jumped to his feet and looked at his right forearm. "If you left a mark, I'm telling."

I continued to sit on the floor, feeling miserable. "You better go home. I think I hear your mom calling."

"Yeah, right, my mom's a mile away at Papago Plaza, right now." He swaggered toward the kitchen so he could leave by the back door.

"See ya Monday, then."

The door slammed behind him.

Monday? That meant he wasn't coming over again until school started. Some friend! I picked up the mangled package. Then, I grabbed the tape dispenser and headed for my room, grateful that my parents' bedroom door was closed again. They were probably wrapping more Christmas gifts.

Inside my room, with the door closed, I hunched over the gift box, tape in hand, but I couldn't resist the urge to peel the paper further back. Inside was a pink Timex watch. My heart sank. Pink? Everyone knew I wouldn't want a girl color! I'd been asking for a watch ever since my birthday, but the one I'd shown Momma had a brown band with a gold face and pointed hands.

I pulled the tape and positioned it, hoping the rip wouldn't show. My brothers liked to shake the packages and guess what was inside, but maybe they'd leave this one alone. I might get away with it unless Poppa rearranged the gifts under the tree. He tended to notice little things that other people missed.

* * *

The next week, I was a little cool toward Terry, not jumping at the chance to go bike riding or hunt lizards after school. I knew he hadn't meant to offend me; he had acted on something that was normal in his family but not in mine. Every year, waiting to find out what presents we got was part of the fun. Now that I knew what my main present was, I was disappointed. I mentioned it to him one day at school.

"Oh, brother, are you still sore about that?"

"You took the specialness out of it," I whined.

"Big deal!"

By Christmas week, I was over it and things were back to normal.

On Christmas Eve, we sat in the family room for our devotions, and with a start I noticed that my present was missing from under the tree. I tried to make everyone think I was looking at the colored lights while I frantically scanned every box I could see, but none was the right shape or size, or had the wrapping paper I remembered! Poppa talked about God's gift of His son, and that the Israelites had waited a long time to receive him. We must be patient to wait for our gifts, too. I almost groaned out loud. Could he see the guilt on my face?

Momma passed a plate of cookies as he continued to speak. "When we jump the gun, sometimes the consequences keep us from enjoying the gift as much as we would have if we'd waited. For instance, remember Thanksgiving, when Gramma brought the cherry pie?"

My brothers groaned and Momma muttered, "Now, Poppa."

"God gives His gifts in His perfect time, and He is joyful when we receive them."

I continued to sit with the family, going through the motions of eating snacks, drinking hot chocolate, and feeling the warm fire as it crackled in the hearth. But by bedtime, I was a nervous wreck. Why had my gift disappeared? Was that my punishment?

* * *

On Christmas morning, we woke up to the smell of waffles, Momma's special holiday treat for us. I dressed slowly, dreading what would happen when we gathered to open presents afterward. At the table, I learned that Gramma had dropped off a pecan pie, which had a small slice out of it... that sat... barely touched... on the kitchen counter. I glanced at it, and Momma shook her head.

"No sugar," she mouthed, and I smiled wanly.

After breakfast, we assembled in the family room, sitting on the floor close to the tree.

Papa began to hand out our gifts, then stopped when he got to me. "Momma—-?"

"Oh, yes!" She jumped up and left the room, returning with a square package, just like the one with the Timex watch, and handed it to me. It had been re-wrapped in different paper. Someone must have figured out what Terry and I had done.

"I hope you like it," she said, tentatively.

As the boys tore into theirs, I pulled at the tape and opened it slowly. Inside was the watch, but it was not the pink one. It was the watch I'd asked for.

"Gee, thanks!" I said with gratitude and relief.

"There's a story behind that," Momma said. Everyone turned toward her to listen. "They didn't have the watch you wanted when I was in the jewelry store, so I had to go back and get it, already wrapped. Then, a week ago I noticed that the paper was sloppy and torn, as if it had been opened and re-wrapped. Why I was so mad at that darn clerk. I could see he wasn't paying attention to what he was doing!

"When I took it back for re-wrapping, I noticed it wasn't even the right watch! They'd given me a pink one. Everyone knows Nellie doesn't like pink. Just then -—you'll never believe it -—Mrs. Maxwell walked in, and she had the wrong watch, too. You know how her little Priscilla likes pink. She'd been given this watch, Nellie, which was meant for you."

By now, tears were streaming down my face. My brothers, Curt and Jim, looked at each other, shaking their heads.

"I got a Beatles scrapbook," Jim whined, mocking me.

"I got a Tonka truck," Curt said in a cry-baby voice.

"All right boys, that's enough," Poppa said. "I'm glad you all enjoyed your gifts, and I hope you will give thanks."

Then, we bowed our heads and gave thanks. And even though everything turned out better than I'd thought it would, I knew I'd never pre-open a gift again.

Orange Moe

6th Grade, January 1967

I usually knew when Terry would go fishing. It had to be a full moon night, and no school the next day. He didn't get to go very often, but when he was done, he'd ride back from Hole-In-The-Rock Park past our farm at five a.m. I couldn't hear the slight clink-clink of the lose bell on his handlebars, but our donkey could, and she started braying. She was our low-cost alarm system.

Awake, lying on my cold linen pillowcase, staring at the bright moon through my window, I'd wait for Terry to enter our gravel driveway. I knew that he carried his rod and some bait with him. And I also knew he never caught anything. I wondered what it would be like to go fishing in the dark, especially in the summer when it was the only time the temperature was below a hundred thirteen.

The prickle of cold on my skin felt good. It was the middle of January, so I knew he'd have on two pairs of sweats, which wouldn't have been enough to keep me warm. But the thing with Terry was, he never got very cold. He told me it was because he was a warm-blooded Italian. I didn't know if this was true or just one of those things parents tell their kids to make them sound special. I thought Italians all had black hair and dark eyes, but Terry had light brown hair and blue eyes. It was true that he didn't get cold easily. And when he did get a little chilly, he would just peddle his bike faster, and that seemed to help.

When the donkey brayed, I knew he was in the semi-circle driveway, and I held my breath until I heard a swoosh as he put his foot down to make a sliding stop in the gravel. I jumped up, threw on my chenille robe and slippers, and snuck through the kitchen to the TV room, even though staying underneath the floral comforter from Aunt Tressie would have felt much better. The funny thing about Terry and fishing was this: even though he never caught a fish, whenever he came back I couldn't wait to ask if he had.

In the TV room, the cold of the linoleum floor penetrated the thin soles of my slippers. I opened the old screen door that didn't quite fit the jamb. It was already unlatched because Jim and Curt were feeding the cows and chickens. I stepped out onto the top cement step, hugging myself to keep warm, and there was Terry, straddling his metallic blue Sting Ray bike. In our neighborhood, a Sting Ray was the coolest bike you could have. It was smaller than a regular bike, with a banana seat and handlebars that came up real high. Perched between the handlebars in the bike basket was a wadded up sweatshirt, and at first I thought he was going to tell me that he caught something. Then I saw it move, and I walked up to the basket where I was greeted with a tiny "mew" and a pair of round golden eyes blinking at me.

"Wow!" I said. "Where'd you get him?"

"He was in your driveway," Terry said. "Lost. He probably needs a bowl of milk or something. You like him?"

I reached into the bike basket where the half-grown orange tabby was swaddled and scooped up the bundle. Another tiny "mew" squeaked out as I cuddled him to my chest and his eyes blinked gratefully.

"You want him?" Terry asked hopefully.

"Sure! How come you don't want him?"

"Aw, my sister's allergic to cats so I already know my mom will say 'no,' but your family has lots of animals, so it shouldn't be any problem for you, huh?"

"Gee, thanks, Terry!"

I held the kitty against my chest, feeling his vibrating purr.

"What're you gonna name him?"

"I don't know yet—-"

"Nellie—-?" Momma's voice called from the kitchen.

"Wanna ride bikes later?" Terry asked.

We looked up at the pale grey sky, streaked with a yellow and pink sunrise. Our mulberry trees, a healthy yellow green in spring and summer, stretched their stark, bare limbs upward.

"Come by after chores," I suggested.

School was out for winter vacation, but I knew I would be helping Momma with housework until well into the afternoon. I slipped in the back door, letting the screen tap softly, and walked into the kitchen where Momma was fixing country breakfast, like she did whenever we were off from school. She made waffles, biscuits, sausage, bacon, eggs, toast, and hot cereal. Jim was considered old enough to drink coffee with breakfast, but to Curt and me it was gross. Jim would chuckle and wink at us, saying, "You'll understand some day."

Momma was already dressed in a plaid house dress. Sleeping cap removed, she'd taken out her pin curls and brushed her brown hair until it was shiny and fluffy. The boys began arguing over who got the first shower. Sometimes the hot water ran out before we all got a chance, so going first was a big deal in the winter. Momma looked over her right shoulder at me while she scrambled the eggs and saw the bundle in my arms.

"What have you got, there?" she asked.

"It's a kitten. Terry found it."

I put the sweatshirt and the cat on the floor, but he didn't move, just looked up at us with his round yellow eyes. I stroked the top of his orange-striped head and the back of his neck and pulled back the sweatshirt. His back leg had a long, thin gash, covered with dried blood and fine dirt. Momma bent down for a closer look.

"I think he's going to be okay," she said. "We'll have the vet take a look at it when he comes by today."

"Can we keep him?"

Momma smiled a yes, so I ran to find an empty cardboard box to make him a bed.

That afternoon, Terry came by at four. It wasn't a good day to ride bikes, so he came over watch TV instead. Just in time for Wallace & Ladmo on channel five, he sailed into the uneven puddles of drizzle in our driveway, spewing dirty gravel up from both sides of his wheels when he stopped. He slammed his bike against the side of our clapboard house and ran up the three cement steps, letting the screen door bang behind him.

"Please wipe your feet," Momma called from the kitchen, even though she knew he wouldn't do it. The linoleum floor in the TV room was easy to clean, so she really didn't care -—she just kept asking him every time, hoping that eventually he would do it.

Terry, mud water slime and all, pounced on the sofa, his long wet bangs flopping on his forehead and coming to rest in his eyes. Wearing bangs in our eyes and shirttails un-tucked was the fad at school because it annoyed our parents and teachers so much. Momma walked in with a plate of warm chocolate chip cookies.

"Terry—-?"

"Yeah!" he cried out involuntarily before he remembered that grown-ups didn't think of 'yeah' as a real word. "I mean, yes, please."

Momma set the plate down on the coffee table near us, then went back into the kitchen for glasses of milk. I walked to the massive TV set, pulled the knob and turned the dial, and heard a slight buzz before the sound of Mike Condello's flute and guitar theme song came on. The Wallace & Ladmo show was a local program featuring grown-ups who talked and acted like kids. They played cartoons and did skits in between them. Wallace was a portly man who wore a wide-striped surf-shirt, a wide tie and a flat straw hat. Ladmo, his sidekick, was tall and skinny and also wore a striped surf-shirt, a long polka dot tie and a tall black tuxedo hat. Ladmo was like a big eager-to-please kid that never quite got what was going on around him, and because of this he often found himself in trouble, due to the antics of Gerald the rich kid. Momma explained to me that Gerald's funny outfit -—an aqua and white striped shirt with a white ruffled collar, bloomers and a curly blond wig -—was a take-off on Little Lord Fauntleroy (whoever that was).

Terry and I gobbled our treats as Gerald pranced onto the screen, ready to spring some new trick on Ladmo.

Gullible as always, and trying to be kind, polite and peaceable, Ladmo said, "That's a nice outfit you're wearing today, Gerald."

"Oh," Gerald said, vamping for the camera. "So, you like my orange moe?"

"Orange moe?" Terry and I said together. "What's that?"

"What's an orange moe?" Ladmo asked, as Wallace walked in.

"Did you hear that?" Gerald stormed. "Can you believe what he just said, Wallace? He's making fun of my clothes!"

"No, no, Wall-boy," Ladmo protested. "I didn't—-"

"What is going on here?" Wallace asked. "Can't I leave you two alone for five minutes without you fighting about something?"

"I just told him I liked his orange moe," Ladmo protested.

"His what?!" Wallace cried.

"If you had gone to private school, as I did -—instead of being one of those public school brats," Gerald said in his snottiest voice, "then you would know that I am speaking with a French accent when I say 'arrangement,' which in French," he continued in a nasally voice, "is pronounced 'orange moe.'"

The music for a cartoon started up as Wallace bopped Ladmo on the head and Ladmo began fake-crying.

"Orange Moe would be a good name for your cat," Terry suggested, and I agreed.

I told him the cat had an injury to his back leg. He may have been trapped somewhere and got hurt trying to escape. When the vet bandaged him up, he'd said it would take a week to heal, but Moe was already doing his best to hobble around the house and explore his new surroundings. I was pleased that he had found a home where he would be well-cared-for. Our whole family agreed to keep him, and after that day his name became Orange Moe.

The next week, we returned to school, the magical wonder of the Christmas holidays fading into memories as we began to concentrate on our studies and rushed through daily assignments so we could rack up as much free time after school as possible. I often played with Terry and his auburn-haired neighbor, Bobby -—making forts, going exploring in the desert, riding bikes and all the other things a tomboy does with her guy friends.

At home, Moe began to gain his strength and after his bandage was removed he bounced all over the house, climbing to the top of the refrigerator, rummaging in closets, and hunting behind the sofa. The vet told us he was about five months old and would have to be fixed soon or his slightly mischievous behavior would get a lot worse because he would start to act like a tom cat. I felt sorry for Moe when I thought about him having surgery, but it turned out to be no big deal, except that he limped around for a few days and couldn't get to the top of the frigde. Toward the end of his recovery period, when he was still pretty calm, the day came for show-and-tell in our science class and I thought it would be fun to bring him to school and talk about him, even though I knew it would not be as exciting as the time Jeff's horse got loose on the playground.

Momma agreed that, since science was my first class of the day, she would drive him to school and take him home. I prepared his cat carrier with a soft towel inside to make him comfortable. Moe didn't seem to mind his confinement. Ever since the day Terry brought him to me, he knew he was my cat and he was happy to be with me wherever I was, whether he was sleeping by my feet in bed at night or resting in my lap while I did homework. The only place he wouldn't go near was the bathtub! Our vet had commented on how calm he was for such a youngster. I decided that -—wherever he came from -—he was grateful for our home.

Momma drove up Rural Road toward school, and passed Terry, Bobby and me pedaling our bikes as fast as we could. At school, we met up with Momma, and she told me she would wait in the car so I could bring Moe back to her after science class. The cage was awkward and heavy, so Terry helped me carry it.

As we walked under the covered outdoor corridor that led toward our classrooms, we attracted a lot of attention. Kids swarmed around, including Debbie Horstbuchen, a dark-haired, dark-eyed girl with a sullen face who would glare when anything upset her. Some kids were so fascinated by her weird expression that they would call her "Debbie's Horse-is-buckin'" to make her glare at them. The Horstbuchen house was on Garfield Avenue, and it was the one house that never got enough attention. Most families had a hard time keeping a lawn green in the Arizona heat, but the Horstbuchens' yard was full of brown, brittle weeds and the paint on their shutters and window frames was chipped and peeling. Debbie saw us with Moe, and she gave the Horstbuchen glare. The hair on Moe's back stood up slightly and he hissed. Terry muttered "weird-o" under his breath as we walked by her.

Mr. Hunting Eagle, our science teacher, was a real American Indian who wore his light brown hair in a Mohawk haircut, even though he dressed like the rest of our male teachers in a short-sleeved shirt and tie. He let me keep Moe's cage on the floor so he wouldn't have to be near the gopher snake, which might have made him nervous. I enjoyed getting up in front of the class and talking about my cat.

Afterward, Terry helped me haul the cat carrier out to the parking lot at the front of the school where Momma waited in the car. We were only halfway down the main corridor when my best friend, Beth, ran up to us.

"Nellie," she warned. "I just saw your momma coming out of the principal's office."

Terry and I looked at each other, wondering what she was doing in there. Principal Brown was a tall, heavy-set man in a black suit and tie, and his main function on campus seemed to be discipline. I had permission to bring Moe to school, so I couldn't imagine what I would be in trouble for, this time.

When I got to the car, Momma didn't say anything except, "Go ahead and put him on the front seat, honey. See you when you get home."

This left me wondering all day why she'd been talking to the principal. I kept trying to push it out of my mind, because I knew if I'd done something really bad the office secretary would come get me out of class.

That day, when Terry and I went to the bike rack for our bikes, we passed Debbie Horstbuchen and she gave us the stare. It added to my apprehension, and Terry noticed how quiet I was as we peddled away from the bike racks in our schoolyard.

"Somethin' buggin' you?" he asked.

Even though I had my hands on the handlebar grips, I shrugged my shoulders.

"Do you ever feel like something bad's about to happen?" was the only way I could explain it.

"I dunno." That was Terry's answer to a lot of questions that didn't have to do with fishing, snakes, or finding new places in the desert to ride our bikes.

When we got to my house, we raced into the semi-circle driveway, as usual, practicing the sliding stop. Terry popped a wheelie. We were beside the family car and I noticed Moe's cage was still sitting on the front seat. The screen door popped open and Momma stood there, wiping her hands on her apron.

Now, Terry knew something was up.

"I gotta go," he said, and pedaled off as fast as he could.

I leaned my bike against the side of the pale green clapboard house and walked toward Momma.

"How come Moe's cage is still in the car?" I asked, my throat constricting.

"Nellie, come in here, please."

"Where is Moe?" my voice squeaked. "Isn't he here?"

"Nellie—-"

I ran past her, not caring that I pushed her slightly as I did.

"Moe!" I cried. "Moe! Kitty, kitty!"

Momma grabbed my shoulders.

"Where is he? What's happened to him?"

"Nellie, sit down—-"

"I have to know!"

"There was a problem at school, today—-"

"Am I being punished for something? Did you take Moe away?"

"Sit down, please."

The back door creaked, followed by a soft bang, as Poppa walked into the room. Now I knew it was serious because he rarely came in early from the fields. He stood beside Momma, so I did as she asked, taking a seat on the couch in the TV room.

"I'm very sorry to tell you this," she began. "It's not your fault. I know that you and Terry found Moe in our yard one morning. But today I learned that Moe already belongs to someone else, so I had to return him."

It took a minute for this to sink in. "Someone else—-?"

"Debbie Horstbuchen. Moe belongs to her."

"He does not! Not that little witch!"

"Nellie—-"

"He's not her cat. He's mine! She's lying!"

"Nellie—-"

"She's lying!"

"Nellie!" Poppa said. "That's enough!"

I got up from the sofa, my shoulders slumped and tears streaming from my eyes. I ran past them, bolted to my room, and slammed the door as hard as I could. It wasn't loud enough, so I slammed it again, to be sure my point was made.

Dinner that night was miserable. It was an okay meal, I guess, but I couldn't taste any of it.

"We can get another cat," Curt said sweetly, his moon face pleasing and kind, like Poppa's.

"I don't want another cat. There's no other cat like him. There will never be another cat like Orange Moe." Then, I turned to my parents, whining. "Don't you remember how he was hurt when we found him? How we made him better?"

Suddenly everyone became very interested in their baked potatoes, so I knew it was no use. I tried to enjoy the corn-on-the-cob Momma made because she knew it was my favorite food. But it was going to be a while before I could be happy again, without Moe.

The weather stayed cold and gloomy, which didn't help my mood. The boys complained about their early mornings, and Terry didn't come over as often. Before Moe was gone, I didn't think about him that much -—I was just happy to know that he was there when I got home from school each day. Now, I thought about him constantly, imagining the sound of his meow at my bedroom window. I went through a phase where I didn't quite know what to do with myself. I noticed all the places in our house that reminded me of something we'd done together -—the time he got stuck on top the fridge; the corner of the TV room where I gave him a saucer of milk during my after-school snack; and even watching Gerald mispronounce French on TV reminded me of how Moe got his name. The house was quieter and emptier without him.

Everyone wanted to help me get over it. Poppa said that it was part of our family history to help wounded animals and strays. Beth said that if you lose something you love, then it wasn't meant to be. Terry, of course, said, "It's just a stupid cat."

One night, I had more homework than usual, so I sat in the TV room reading when I heard the soft tapping of the back screen door against the door jamb. At first, I ignored it, because I knew one of the boys had forgotten to latch the screen and when the wind caught it just right, it would flap open and shut. Then I heard something unexpected: "Meyow."

I jumped up from my books, knocking them off the coffee table.

"Moe! Moe's home!" I cried as I ran to the back door.

Soon everyone was standing behind me as I opened it, cried out loud, and scooped him up in my arms. He was dusty and dirty, but snuggled me back, his fuzzy orange face nudging mine. I brought him in and closed the door. Momma and Poppa looked at each other.

"What's that on his tail?" Curt asked.

We all looked and saw something dark.

"Oil—-?"

Moe allowed me to hold him as the boys examined him. They looked at each other in silent agreement but said nothing. We all knew it was blood.

"Now can we keep him?" I asked.

Poppa slowly walked to my pet and touched his tail in the dark area. Moe struggled slightly in my arms.

"This animal has been abused," Poppa said. "We will keep him."

When Monday came, I was pretty nervous. Terry and I pedaled to school, and on our way we passed Debbie Horstbuchen. This time, she didn't stare at us, just walked with her head down.

"Weird-o!" Terry hissed as we rode by.

When she looked up, I saw dark circles under her eyes and she was holding one arm in the other.

"Don't say that," I scolded him, after the fact.

"She stole your cat. She deserves it."

"No, she doesn't. I'm the one who's going to win after Poppa talks to Principal Brown. You don't have to rub it in."

Terry ignored me, and slowed his bike down so he could pop a good wheelie. Poppa drove by in his pick-up, and when we went to the bike racks to lock our bikes up for the day, I watched him stride toward Principal Brown's office. He would look out of place there in his denim overalls and Pendleton shirt. Terry whistled the theme song of *Batman* and we chuckled in anticipation of Poppa's success.

When the lunch bell sounded and we streamed out of our classes to the cafeteria, we saw something unexpected. Debbie Horstbuchen was being led by her teacher to a waiting police car.

"Wow!" Terry said. "I didn't know you could get into that much trouble over stealing a cat!"

When I got home from school that day, I gave Moe a can of tuna to show him how much I loved him. There was a festive mood in the house, a feeling of triumph. At dinnertime, Poppa came in from the field and walked straight into the kitchen where he talked to Momma in a low voice. I heard him say "tell her" and Momma say "tell her" and I knew they were talking about me, but the tone of their voices was somber. I held Moe close, afraid they'd take him away again.

When dinner was ready, we all came to the table and sat down.

"What happened at school today?" Curt asked me. "I saw a police car."

Poppa took his time answering. "Well, it's something very unfortunate. Sometimes there are people who shouldn't be parents."

I looked at Curt and he looked at me: What the heck did that mean?

"It's a good thing Moe came back here," Poppa continued, "because it actually served as a warning. When I reported to the principal that the cat had been abused, he called in Debbie Horstbuchen, and discovered that she had a broken arm."

"She came to school with a broken arm?" Curt exclaimed. "Why didn't her parents take her to the doctor?"

"Well, that's just it, you see," Poppa continued tactfully. "It was her dad who hurt her."

"How did he do that?" Jim wanted to know.

"I don't know, son," Poppa answered. "Sometimes a mom or dad isn't a fit parent. When they get angry with their child, instead of counting to ten or having some cooling-off time, they lash out in anger and injure their child."

I suddenly felt very low. "So, you mean Debbie got beat up by her own dad?"

"Something like that," he answered uncomfortably. "For now, she will be put in safe custody, then the Court will decide whether she can go back and live with her parents again."

Now, I felt bad for all the times we'd made fun of Debbie Horstbuchen. I even felt bad that she'd lost Moe. He must have tried to comfort her, just as he did with me. But then I didn't feel that bad because I knew that if Debbie wasn't safe in her home, then Moe wasn't safe there, either.

"Is there anything we can do," Momma asked, "for the girl, or her family?"

"Only one thing I can think of," said Poppa. "Jim? Nellie? Curt?"

"Pray?" I asked timidly.

"Yes. We will pray for that little girl's safety."

A few days later, Terry and Bobby, the auburn-haired kid, rode over to tell me that there was a "for sale" sign in the Horstbuchens' front yard, and no car in the driveway. My family and I continued to pray for the unknown future of Debbie.

"Who Is Itt?"

7th Grade, October 1967

"Guess what I'm gonna be?"

Terry whizzed by me on his metallic blue Sting Ray bike, his auburn-haired neighbor Bobby trailing behind us. Both wore button down plaid shirts and corduroy pants. No denim allowed on our school campus.

Terry was referring to the yearly Halloween party where our one room cafeteria with its high ceiling would turn into a haunted house full of costumed kids. This year would be different for us. Now that we were in seventh grade, we were invited to attend the dance afterward. I looked forward to it, hoping that the new kid, Ricky Hodge, would ask me to dance.

"What are you gonna be?" I pedaled faster. Riding in a skirt wasn't that bad once you got used to it.

"Cousin Itt!" Terry cried over his shoulder as I gained on him.

Bobby trailed behind us.

"From the TV show?" I asked. "It's not on anymore."

As soon as I said it, I knew he'd be sore. He turned to look at me, his light brown bangs flopped against his forehead. Bobby was now even with us as we rode in a pack like The Three Muskateers. He looked straight ahead. He didn't want any of Terry's quick temper landing on him.

"So what? It's still a cool costume. It's all hair. My idea is so groovy everyone will wish they'd thought of it first," Terry bragged, his eyes straight ahead, though few cars drove down the street this time of day. "My mom's gonna help me. It will take a sheet, an old mop and lots of yarn. You can laugh now if you want, but I'm gonna win the costume contest."

"Boss," Bobby said.

It was the new "in" word and it sounded even better than cool or groovy.

We rode south on 68th Street until Terry and Bobby peeled off on Taylor. I continued toward home, flying down the dip in the road and coasting halfway up the other side, my shoulder length brown hair flapping behind me. I had been thinking about my looks all day and couldn't wait to call Beth on the phone so we could plan our costumes, make-up, and hairstyles for the dance.

When I got to the light green clapboard house at the end of the semi-circle gravel driveway, I slammed my bike down and ran through the back door. Momma, in the kitchen, watched me pass the TV room and raised her eyebrows.

"No Wallace and Ladmo show with Terry, today?"

"Nope."

I rushed to my bedroom and my new princess phone. It was just like Beth's, except hers was pink. I closed the door then stopped and leaned against it to catch my breath, remembering something Momma said recently: "The day will come when you and Terry will get tired of watching Wallace and Ladmo cartoons after school."

She was right. Even though Terry and I still rode bikes to and from school most days, he had stopped coming over regularly. He rode home with Bobby instead of coming over and begging Momma for cookies.

I shed my matching skirt and blouse in favor of jeans and a T-shirt, then flopped onto my bed, smothered in the floral comforter Aunt Tressie had given me. Propped against a couple of pillows, I dialed my best friend's number. Her words came out in a rush; I could hardly follow what she was saying.

"Who's the note from?" I asked her when I could get a word in edgewise.

I pictured my best friend sitting on her ruffled pink bedspread. She had long blonde hair to her waist and she curled it at the ends. Her family had more money than most of ours did, so her clothes came from the major department stores in Phoenix. She was also allowed to wear lipstick, even though it was only light pink. Beth Peterson was the prettiest and most popular girl in the seventh grade.

"I don't know who it's from. Want me to read it to you?"

"Yeah!"

"Dear Beth: Your hair is pretty. I like you a lot. Signed, question mark."

"Question mark? Who's that?"

"I don't know. When I got to math class, I saw it stuck in my desk -—you know how the arm rest curves around, and you can put your books and stuff underneath on that little wire shelf?"

"Uh-huh." I pressed the phone to one ear and dangled my legs over the edge of my bed, stretching them, looking at my socks.

"And the arm rest is where you can put your right arm?"

"Yeah, unless you have a left-handed desk."

"But who has one of those?" I pictured her rolling her eyes as she said it.

"Southpaws."

"Oh, yeah. Anyway, you interrupted me."

"Oh, sorry. Go on."

"Well, right by where my right elbow goes—-"

"Right by your right—-?"

We both giggled.

"Yeah, right by my right where I write."

I giggled. Not because it was funny. It was the forced giggle all Beth's friends made. We never told her when her jokes were corny.

"The note was stuck in there."

"No one else saw it? The teacher didn't see it?"

"No, it was small. Like, remember when we were in third grade and we made Cootie Catchers?"

"So, your secret admirer is a third grader?" I teased. I flopped to another position on my saggy bed. "You guys will look funny at the dance when he rests his head on your elbow for the slow ones."

"No—-!" she exclaimed in a further fit of giggles. I could picture what she was doing now, lying on her back and kicking her feet up. "Anyway, third graders aren't that short."

"So, you would dance with one?"

"No!!!" she laughed even harder. "I was trying to make you remember Cootie Catchers."

"Yeah, I remember."

"Well, the note was folded up like that. He took a full sheet of notebook paper and folded it into a small triangle."

"Wow! And he only signed it with a question mark?"

"Yeah, and I don't have his fingerprints," she said sarcastically.

"But don't you have Mrs. Roycroft for math class?" I asked. Picturing the tall extra-wide teacher with the poodle haircut was enough to make me shudder.

"Yes."

"She's strict. If she finds out someone's passing notes—-"

"I know. But it shows that my secret admirer has guts."

"You can say that again."

"It shows that my—-"

"Just kidding."

Beth laughed. "I have to find out who it is. Is it some guy I like, or some creep-o?"

"Who do you like?"

There was a pause.

"Beth?"

"Well, several guys are kind of cute."

"Like -—?"

"Like Dave Jones. Like Alex Thomas. Like Terry."

"Terry?!" I couldn't believe it. Beth thought my sweaty bike-riding buddy was cute?

"I know you can't see it, Nellie, because he's like a brother to you. But some of us think he's cute."

What could I say to that? Terry? Cute?

"C'mon, Nellie, stop being a tomboy and be a girl. Isn't there someone you like?"

I stayed quiet.

"Come on!"

"Well," I confessed, "at first I thought Bobby Robbins was cute, until I found out he was a chicken. One day, me and Terry and Bobby were riding our bikes in the desert and we stopped to throw rocks at a scorpion and Bobby was so scared he started to cry. He thought it would charge us and run up his leg and sting him. We killed it, though."

The line was silent for a minute, then I heard a click.

"Party line," Beth said.

"Oh, yeah."

"We're still talking," she informed the other party.

The line clicked again.

"So, anyway," Beth said, "Bobby Robbins doesn't count if you thought he was a chicken and you made him cry."

"I didn't make him cry! He did it to himself."

"Oh, so what. Tell me a boy you think is cute, that you actually like."

"Ricky Hodge," I mumbled.

"Who?"

"The new kid in my English class."

"I don't know who he is yet," Beth said.

We talked for at least another hour. She wanted to know all about the color of Ricky's hair (brown), his eyes (hazel), how tall he was (about 5'6", not much taller than me), and what he usually wore (tan corduroy pants and a brown corduroy jacket). During this drawn-out conversation, the party line clicked on several more times and I finally asked Beth who it was, but she didn't know. I wondered if they were listening in, and we giggled about that, thinking how funny it would be if we made up fake stories so the snooper would spread it around and get in trouble.

Then we fantasized about what it would be like when we were old enough to have a slumber party -—what games we'd play, and who we'd invite. We stayed on the phone until it was time for supper at my house.

* * *

The next day when I went to the school cafeteria for lunch I couldn't find Beth, so I sat with Karen and Laurie. Karen was a laid-back, sweet-voiced girl with honey blonde hair and blue eyes. Laurie was a warm, friendly, heavy-set girl with shoulder length brown hair and brown eyes. They didn't know where Beth was, either, but we knew she was at school because we'd all seen her after first period.

"Alex Thomas walked her to school today," Karen told us.

Just then, Beth approached our table holding her lunch tray out in front of her, walking like a robot. She wasn't clowning around. Her face was drawn, and she sat down without a word, staring at her food.

"What's wrong?" I asked.

I could tell she was trying not to cry.

Two eighth graders walked by.

"Beth got in trouble," they jeered.

A tear slid down her cheek and she brushed it away with the back of her hand.

"What happened?" I asked.

"It's that mean Mrs. Roycroft," she said. "She made me stay after class for ten minutes!" She choked and took a sip of milk. "It's not my fault. I didn't do anything!"

We all looked at each other, waiting for her to explain. She picked up her fork and poked the Salisbury steak that looked like a reject from a TV dinner.

Terry and Bobby walked by.

"Have fun in math class, today?" Terry said and kept walking.

Beth turned red.

"What happened?" we chorused.

"Well, some boy wrote me a note yesterday. And today, when I walked to my desk—-" she stopped, still choking a little, "-—there were a million notes piled up on my desk chair. The teacher blamed me, but I don't know anything about it!"

"What kind of notes?" Laurie asked.

"Love notes." Beth spat out the words like they were a mouthful of brussel sprouts. "'I love you, Beth.' 'Will you be mine?' The whole class was laughing at me."

She burst into tears.

* * *

Though there had been days that I'd raced home from school and not been greeted by the smell of fresh baked cookies, this was the first day I was overly aware of it. My afternoon had been strange. Beth, preoccupied, had not passed notes to me in last period, and Terry did not meet me at the bike racks to race home. Instead, I saw him talking to Beth in front of the school before her mom picked her up, but they didn't see me. I pedaled home alone and walked into an empty kitchen.

I could hear Momma in her bedroom as she talked on the phone. When she came out and saw me, she looked surprised. She brushed her medium length brown hair back away from her forehead and reached down to smooth the skirt of her pastel house dress.

"Hello, dear."

"No cookies?"

"Not today. But I do have a treat for you. I have to go to TG&Y, so I thought I'd take you with me and we'd stop at Revco for triple-dip cones."

I didn't really want to go with her on her errand but three scoops of ice cream was hard to pass up. We drove to Papago Plaza, an outdoor shopping mall near where Beth lived. I knew Momma wanted to have a serious talk with me because that's what she usually did when she drove me somewhere. When I was locked in the car with her, I couldn't get away.

"Did you have a problem with Beth today?" she asked, glancing to the side to see my reaction.

"A problem?" My mouth went dry.

Her eyes returned to the road and its sparse traffic. "Mrs. Peterson called me. She said Beth is very upset with you."

"Upset with me? Why?"

"She said you told her secret."

"What secret?"

"Something about a note from a boy who likes her."

"I didn't tell anybody about that. She didn't say it was a secret, but I didn't tell anyone."

"Not even Terry?"

"Especially not Terry! Why would I tell a boy? They don't care about that stuff."

"You're right, Nellie. I told Mrs. Peterson you would never repeat Beth's secrets. But we were trying to figure out how all the boys knew about it. She didn't tell anyone but you and a few other girls."

I shadowed Momma through TG&Y, then tried to act enthusiastic at the ice cream counter at Revco. Momma complained about how there wasn't enough yarn at TG&Y to keep going on her Christmas afghan while I thought about Beth and her problems.

"We're going to have to figure out a costume for you," Momma said after she ordered our cones.

"I want to go as a pirate, like last year."

The two ladies at the counter, in their mint green nylon dresses, white starched aprons and teased hair, continued talking as they scooped our ice cream.

"Well, on a party line, you can hear everything," one of them told the other.

I grabbed Momma's arm. "That's it! The party line! Someone eavesdropped on Beth and me! I'd sure like to find out who."

"Well, that should be easy," Momma said. "It has to be one of her neighbors."

* * *

I couldn't wait to call Beth so we could play detective about the party line, but because she got in trouble at school she wasn't allowed to talk on the phone. The next time I saw her was in the cafeteria the following day at noon, flanked by Laurie and Karen. Their lunch trays were pushed to the side because they were hunched over something, so absorbed that they didn't notice me until I scooted onto the bench seat facing them.

"What are you looking at?" I asked.

All three raised their heads at the same time and jabbered excitedly. "It's another note from the secret admirer."

Beth pushed it toward me, and I read it quickly: "Beth, I am too shy to tell you how much I like you, but I am going to tell you at the Halloween dance. You will know me by my costume -—Cousin Itt."

I tried not to let my face show what I was thinking. So, Terry was the one who was writing the love notes!

* * *

Terry and Bobby were waiting for me after school at the bike racks. In my mind, I had already decided that if Terry had a crush on Beth there was no reason for him to hang around me, unless he was using me to get closer to her. I didn't want to be a jerk about it, but let's just say this wasn't my friendliest bike ride home with Terry. And, knowing me as well as he did, he knew something was wrong but he didn't want to hear what it was.

At dinner that night, I was still in a fog, trying to imagine that two of my best friends might become... boyfriend and girlfriend. Poppa came to the table and took his cap off, setting it on a nearby armchair. His hair stayed plastered to his head where the cap had been.

It was already dark out and my brothers buzzed with excitement because tomorrow was Halloween. My younger brother, Curt, wore his skeleton costume to the table, then pushed the round plastic face mask back on top his head so he could eat. He was blonde and blue-eyed with a round friendly face. Poppa said the blessing, then we began to pass the food and talk about our day.

"I had to drive into Scottsdale, today," Poppa told Momma, "so I dropped by TG&Y to see if I could find any more yarn for you."

Momma looked at him hopefully.

"What a mess!" Poppa exclaimed. "I've never seen Papago Plaza so busy before Halloween! There was a line outside TG&Y. I decided to wait, but -—no luck. Apparently, they're out of yarn and mops. Everybody was complaining."

I bit my tongue. Yarn and mops?

"Yeah," Curt said casually, "that's because a lot of the seventh-grade boys are dressing up as Cousin Itt. They make the costume using a sheet, then their moms sew a mop on top of it and tie on a bunch of yarn to make it look like hair."

"A lot of seventh-grade boys are wearing a Cousin Itt costume?" I stammered.

"What's the point of that?" my high-school age brother, dark-haired skinny Jim, asked with a chuckle.

"Someone's playing a joke," Curt said. "I don't know who started it, but someone got the Cousin Itt idea and everybody thought it would be funny to..."

I rushed through my dinner, tuning out the rest of the conversation. Terry was going to be hopping mad when he found out about this.

No one in my family noticed when I snuck out the back door and picked up my bike. We weren't supposed to ride after twilight because we didn't have bike lights, but there were very few cars out after dark. The stores were all closed, and there was really no place to go. I knew if I was careful I could zip over to Terry's to warn him of the problem and be back in my room before anyone knew I'd gone out.

His house looked like most of the other tract homes on Taylor Street. The porch light was off, but lights shone through the picture window in the living room so I knocked on his front door. He came outside where we hunched together and whispered. My story spilled out and he cocked his head to one side as he listened, thinking.

"Rat finks!" he swore. "I don't know who did this to me, but I'll get even. I'm gonna win the costume contest."

"What about the note to Beth?" I forced myself to ask him. "Did you send it?"

"What note?" he asked, distracted.

"Beth got another love note, from someone who said they would be wearing a Cousin Itt costume."

"Well, it wasn't me!"

"I just can't figure out how everyone found out."

"Well, you said Beth has a party line."

"Yes..."

"Well, don't you know who lives next door to her?"

"No, who?"

"Alex Thomas! I'll fix that guy," he muttered as I retreated back to my bicycle.

This was turning into a big mess.

* * *

The next day at school was the perfect day for the Halloween party and dance. Just like every year at this time, the daytime temperature was in the forties, and our schoolyard trees scattered their dead leaves across the ground. We crunched through them, mashing as many as possible. The outside corridors filled with younger kids wearing costumes and carrying grocery sacks or pillowcases to put their candy in.

I wanted to tell Beth everything I knew but I never got the chance. At the lunch table, instead of just Laurie and Karen hanging around, there were several other girls, and they were all talking at once about costumes and make-up and who they wanted to dance with. Beth was the center of attention as she told her stories about the love notes and how her secret admirer was going to wear a Cousin Itt costume so she would know who he was. There was no way I could easily break in to let her know what my brother Curt said -—that a lot of seventh-grade boys would be dressed as Cousin Itt. Which one would come forward to dance with Beth?

Names were thrown out as people tried to solve the mystery. Who was "Itt"? Was it Alex Thomas? Dave Jones? Terry? Bobby? Or even Ricky Hodge? I listened without saying a word and no one noticed.

Seventh and eighth graders were released from school early that day, at two o'clock, so we could go home and change clothes for the party and dance. The kids serving on student council, which included Beth, began decorating, taping crepe paper streamers to the ceiling and covering the windows with black construction paper.

When I returned to school a little later in my pirate costume, a hairy white Cousin Itt with a huge cardboard sign stood at the door to admit me. The sign, attached to a two-by-four, read "Dogpile on the Rabbit," in green, orange and purple glitter. This was something one of our local DJs on KRIZ said, but I didn't know what it meant or why everyone laughed when he said it.

"Go on in," the Itt said in Terry's cheerful voice.

No one else was nearby, so I asked him, "Why do you have that sign?"

If I could have seen through all the yarn, I would have seen Terry smile. "I'm gonna win this contest, you just watch."

It was early, so there weren't that many people inside yet. Everybody could tell who I was, even with my black eye patch. I wandered among the younger kids for a few minutes, then entered the horror maze where a bowl of cold spaghetti was a dead man's guts, and peeled grapes were eyeballs. The little kids squealed, but of course this wasn't the first time I'd been to one of these.

When I emerged from the maze, the darkened room was full of kids. Beth was in a Rapunzel costume, near the stage. She didn't look happy.

I walked to her side. "What's wrong, me pretty?" I said in pirate talk.

"Look at that," she pointed.

I looked toward the middle of the large room, where the dancing would start as soon as the music came on. My eyes adjusted, and I saw clearly that there were at least twenty boys in Cousin Itt costumes. I knew they were all boys because I could see their pants and shoes under the edge of their sheets. They looked like ghosts covered in long strands of yarn. Each carried a cardboard sign with Magic Marker letters that read, "Dogpile on the Rabbit."

"I don't get it..." I said.

Beth crossed her arms and pouted. "Someone found out about my secret admirer, and now it's just another joke on me. First, he said he would dress up as Cousin Itt and after the dance he would tell me who he was. Then, he wrote me another note because he found out that a bunch of the boys were going as 'Itt,' so he said he was going to carry a sign. Well, those boys must have found out about it, because they're all carrying the same stupid sign. How will I ever know which boy likes me?"

I wanted to tell her, "They all do," but I said nothing.

"This has been the rottenest week. What else will go wrong?" she grumbled.

One of our teachers got up on stage and instructed the younger kids to go home, then directed the dance music to start. It was the first time I'd ever been to a dance. Beth was approached immediately, and she danced with several of the Itts and a number of other guys, as I watched. A few of them asked me, but I didn't want to. I was only interested in Ricky Hodge but I couldn't find him in the crowd. He was either one of the Itts or he'd decided not to come. Eventually, I noticed him, dressed up as a farmer. I looked his way a couple of times, but I never caught his eye and the dance continued from song to song for two hours until it was time to judge the costumes.

Mr. Gonzalez took the stage. He was one of our youngest teachers and was very popular. He had brown hair and a thick moustache. Our other male teachers didn't have facial hair. But they all wore ties with their shirts, and he did, too. That was the rule.

"Well, this has been a very hard contest to judge," he announced. "There are many interesting costumes here today, but I am intrigued that about twenty of you boys all dressed up in the same one——Cousin Itt from the Addams Family." Kids cheered. "Very clever, and I can only remind you of the saying, 'Great minds think alike.' I'll bet there are a lot of local moms who are pretty upset that TG&Y is out of mops and yarn." Everyone laughed. "The student council has taken a vote, and of course it was unanimous that Cousin Itt is the winning costume. But in order to award the prize, which is two extra-large pizzas at the Pizza Parlor, we need your help. So, I want all of the Cousin Itts to come up and stand in a row in front of the stage for the final judging."

Twenty-two boys of various shapes and sizes lined up facing the room. Most of the fake-hair costumes were made from whitish yarn, but I guess when the store ran out, some of them had to switch to tan and brown. White, of course, was most like the real Cousin Itt on TV. Each of the Itts held a "Dogpile on the rabbit" sign but Terry's was the only fancy one. Mr. Gonzalez held his hand over each contestant's head and asked for applause. Terry was clearly the winner and stepped forward to collect his prize.

There was one final dance song, a slow one, "A Whiter Shade of Pale" by Procol Harum. I was standing near Beth when Ricky Hodge walked up to ask her for a dance.

"No, thank you," she said.

He turned away quickly to hide his embarrassment.

Then, Terry came over. Beth and Terry stood facing each other for a minute, without a word. Finally, Beth said, "Were you the one who wrote me those notes?"

Terry snickered. "Naw, it wasn't me. I just know who caused all the trouble by spreading rumors. It was Alex Thomas."

"How do you know that?" Beth shot back.

"I have my ways," he said smugly.

He reached under his sheet costume into his pants pocket and took out a small, folded triangle of notebook paper and held it out. She looked at it, then looked up at the eye holes in his costume, barely visible behind the mop and the yarn hair. I watched her face change as thoughts flashed through her mind. Terry just said he didn't write the love notes, but he was handing her a note that looked just like them. She snatched it from him and unfolded it hastily so she could read it.

When she finished, she looked up at him, her eyes searching for some expression even though his face was covered. I knew Terry like the back of my hand, and I was sure he was grinning behind his straggly mop costume.

"Who gave you this?" she finally asked.

"Dave Jones."

Beth and I looked at each other in surprise. Dave Jones was the shyest boy in our class.

Terry straightened his sheet costume then turned and walked off. His interest in the matter was over. Beth and I forgot that it was the last dance number and hurried to the girls' restroom together.

Once inside the small room with one toilet, she turned on the light and locked the door. She handed the note over to me, and I read it: "Dear Beth, I'm sorry someone wrecked my plan to dance with you today. But I will try again at the Sadie Hawkins dance."

We wondered whether the note really was from Dave or if Terry was playing a trick on us, but Beth said the handwriting looked the same. We stared at it in exasperation. The Sadie Hawkins dance was a whole month away.

The Overnight

9th Grade, November 1969

I never thought of my best friend, Beth, as the kind of girl who was headed for trouble. But, trouble can be so many different things. There's the harmless kind -—like ditching class one day to see what it felt like and then getting caught -—and then there's the kind that lasts a lot longer, when one bad decision leads to a bigger one. Sometimes the wrong decision doesn't seem that bad at the time, but the next one is worse. I think that's what happened with her.

When we were still in grade school, there was plenty to keep us busy, and I don't remember ever feeling bored. But high school was different. On the one hand, it was more exciting than we had imagined -—older kids, younger teachers, rumors of pot-smoking and teenage pregnancy. On the other hand, we were faced with certain limitations -—our menstrual cycles. I no longer had the ability to run, jump, play as I once had, because one week a month (or longer, sometimes) was now reserved for a pain level that even Midol couldn't completely obliterate. In addition to the constant vigilance paid to our wardrobe on those "days of the month," we had to invent believable excuses as to why we "couldn't" attend a dance, or go swimming, or even hang around at the Pizza Parlor after school. We didn't know how much Boys knew about how we felt. We were all forced to take the facts-of-life class together, so we knew that They knew about our periods, but secretly we hoped they didn't know about Our periods.

Yet, out of our new-found liberation -—with chains attached -—came something I'd never experienced before: boredom. Things that Beth and I had been amused by several years ago were now things we were embarrassed to admit we'd ever done or talked about doing. Our beloved Barbie doll collections, with their elaborate hand-sewn costumes, were shoved to the back of high closet shelves or sold for a dime at a yard sale, and our once-shiny bicycle chains rusted from neglect. The ranch life that had seemed so special and unique had become a hindrance -—I couldn't walk down our driveway in sling back pumps without the gravel chewing up the delicate heels. Now, I had to either persuade my big brother Jim to give me a lift to school or I had to wear my tennis shoes and ditch them in someone's bushes so I could walk into class in my high heels.

Beth met me at the army green lockers in the hall by the drama department with a smile that always meant, "I have exciting news."

And it was exciting news. Her youth group was having a retreat, an overnight by bus to a big church on the west side of town. This would be our first time away from home on our own, without our parents.

"And," her blue eyes sparkled, "boys will be there."

"Boys from our class?"

"No, Stupid, Boys-from-Phoenix."

Even though I hated it when Beth called me "Stupid," I was too interested to get mad. I somehow imagined that Boys-from-Phoenix didn't have the pimples, the greasy hair, the braces and the poorly adjusted glasses that the boys from our school had. And, for the rest of my afternoon classes, I had visions of tall boys who would speak with confidence about music, drama, poetry, art. They would realize we were their equals in coolness, and they would use double-entendres to show their interest in us. They would look like Davy Jones or Bobby Sherman, have the wit of Tom Lehrer or Ogden Nash, but with the sophisticated personalities of Napoleon Solo or Illya Kuryakin. Like Beth, I couldn't wait to meet them.

The church bus was an old metal light blue relic from the 1940's with scratchy brown upholstered seats and unpredictable springs that squeaked sometimes when we turned a corner. Mrs. Casaverde sat near us. She was a thin brunette with a shoulder length flip, freckles and big brown eyes, who wore a tomato red v-neck sweater and a plaid wool skirt. As the unheated bus -—smelling of diesel fuel and motor oil -—bounced along the two-lane asphalt highway, past grapefruit orchards and an occasional cement-and-stucco office building, the sun descended, reminding us it was five-thirty and that we would get to eat soon.

Mrs. Casaverde was trying to get some of us to sing, starting with "Cumbaya", and Beth -—surrounded by the cool crowd -—was making hand gestures, pointing to her hair and then her finger. Even though there was nothing in her hair, we knew what she was telegraphing -—"bow, ring" -—as her entourage, Laurie and Anita, tittered. Laurie and Anita hadn't been friends with Beth as long as I had, and they were just school friends who didn't come to her house on weekends like I did. Beth had reached a point in life where she wanted to be the center of a group, and these two girls wanted to be in that group.

Beth, with her long blonde hair curled slightly at the end, her snapping blue eyes and straight white teeth, was still one of the prettiest girls in school, even though in high school there were a lot more girls to compete with. Laurie and Anita wanted to be like her, but Laurie's overweight figure and shy demeanor, and Anita's black frizzy hair, thick glasses, acne and sarcastic personality kept them in Beth's shadow, which was right where Beth wanted them to be. Laurie never realized that with a little dieting and some cosmetics, her lush brown hair and soft brown eyes would easily attract boys. And Anita, if she started using Phisohex, and toned down her need to give an opinion on everything, could probably attract a boyfriend, too. As for me and boyfriends -—well, I was still wearing my dark brown hair in a short, practical shag and I often forgot to put on my mascara. The difference was, I didn't care that much.

Mrs. Casaverde didn't seem to notice Beth's antics and began another round of singing with "Michael Rowed His Boat Ashore". Then, as all the girls began to settle down, she told a story I'd heard Poppa tell many times over dinner, a story about a sheep that gets separated from its flock and how the shepherd leaves all the other sheep just so he can find the lost one.

I stole a look at Beth, who was fake snoring to let us know that she was so bored she could no longer stay awake. One girl laughed nervously. The rest of us stayed quiet. Mrs. Casaverde then offered her prayer: "Lord, this bus is filled tonight with Your precious lambs. Please help all the teachers to provide guidance to any sheep who may have become lost."

When she said "Amen," a dull buzz traveled through the bus, from front to back, picking up momentum as we realized we were getting closer to our destination, and dinner.

"You guys!" Beth grabbed my arm, sinking her slender paint-chipped nails into my forearm. "Look!" she hissed, pointing out the window.

Walking on the shoulder beside us was a tall, skinny guy with long dishwater blond hair like the lead singer in Herman's Hermits.

"Cool," she said.

"He's smoking," Anita said.

"But look at what he's smoking," Beth said.

The bus passed by the spindly teen in the tight blue jeans and grey sweatshirt.

"What?" Laurie asked.

Beth whispered something.

"What?"

"What?"

We all wanted to know.

"He's smoking pot," Beth said in a slightly louder whisper.

We all practically climbed into her lap to crane our necks past her face, hands cupped against the dry-cold window. But the darkening sky, and his receding figure, kept us from seeing much more than a shadowy shape with a glowing red dot by his mouth.

"He is not," Anita said.

"Is, too," Beth said.

"How would you know?"

Beth formed her lips into a smug smile. "I could tell by the way he was holding it in his fingers, in between his teeth. That's how they do it."

"Dope is for dopes," Laurie said.

"I'm not a dope," Beth protested.

"Good thing for that," I agreed.

"Have you tried it, Beth?" Anita challenged.

"No..." Beth answered slowly.

"Would you?"

The bus made a sharp right turn into a dirt and gravel parking lot, throwing us into Beth's lap, again.

"Get off me!" she squealed, giggling.

We piled to the front of the bus and down the metal steps in a lump, pouring into a parking lot whose temperature was forty degrees and dropping quickly.

"Who has my coat?" someone called from behind us.

"Girls, girls," Mrs. Casaverde said. "Line up and follow me."

This church was so different from my family's church. Our church was a modern, A-frame building with a beamed ceiling and space-age lighting. This church was made from large, carved stones cemented together under a gabled roof. The stained glass windows held vibrant blues, reds and golds in lead casements. The pews were lined with soft moss-green velvet cushions.

Solemnly, we walked through the chapel and out one of the side doors into a large room that had been added on after the church was built, though it was still really old. It had heavy wood window frames and a steam-heating radiator in the corner. It was filled with overstuffed furniture like the kind my Grandma had, big and boxy with wooden claw feet. We began to dump our quilts and overnight cases on the once-plush floral carpeting.

Then, after we'd laid our things down, claiming a spot by the radiator or the windows or the door, we were led to the dining hall, a newer building behind the church, with linoleum floors, walls painted a glossy canary yellow, and florescent lights suspended from the ceiling with chains. One of the teachers was explaining that this room was used for a program to feed and house needy families during the winter months. The program would begin Monday, and that was why Teen Winter Camp was held the weekend before.

Several hundred kids poured in as we grabbed seats at the benches and tables, aluminum versions of the popular old redwood picnic tables. A Sunday School Teacher stood at the front of the room trying to give directions nobody could hear. Beth pointed to her hair, her finger——and her hand stopped in mid-air. Her mouth started to open in surprise, then she popped her jaw shut. We looked in the direction she was staring and there he was -—the pot smoker, joining a large group of teenage boys.

What Beth did next was embarrassing. The look on her face, one we all knew too well, boasted, "Watch this."

She stood up and worked her way through the room as skillfully as a fish navigates stones in a streambed. By now, tables of kids were being instructed to line up for their dinner trays, and Beth was swallowed up among the strangers. We looked at each other, not sure what to do.

Anita stood up and announced, "This is not where I sit on the sidelines," and walked in Beth's direction at a fast clip, gently elbowing people aside when necessary.

Laurie and I looked at each other and shrugged. We sensed we would be on our own for the rest of the evening. A loud shriek brought all talking in the room to a stop, as everyone turned toward Beth, the front of her sweater covered with Sloppy Joe sauce, as she looked sheepishly at her newfound beau and cried out, "Oooops, sorry!" Only Beth would think of wearing a light blue mohair sweater on an overnight trip, and only Beth would sacrifice that sweater to meet a boy she thought was cute.

After dinner, we were sent back to our sleeping areas for warmer clothes because the next part of the evening would be spent in front of a campfire. When Laurie and I found the place we'd dropped our quilts, we saw that Beth and Anita had already come and gone. Beth's beautiful chili-stained sweater rested on top her pillow.

"We won't have any trouble finding our way in the dark," Laurie quipped. "All we have to do is find the Sloppy Joe smell."

I was beginning to like her more already.

Behind the chapel, there was a large grass field, slick with frost, so we walked carefully, bundled up in our warmest pants, jackets, caps and gloves. There was a large fire pit built of cement blocks, and the boys were feeding the fire to make it as high as possible. Scattered nearby were some aluminum picnic tables, and some kids spread blankets across them so they'd be warm enough to sit on. Teachers walked around with huge bags of marshmallows, including the pastel-colored ones, and boys walked around with sticks they'd pulled off the nearby mulberry trees. A few kids played guitars and sang.

Laurie and I stopped, standing close together on the frosty field, scanning the crowd of two hundred kids in search of Beth and Anita. It was hard enough to find people you know in the dark, and even harder when their faces were covered up with hats and scarves. From a distance, every kid looked alike. Finally, Laurie touched my arm and pointed. Beth and the pot smoker were sitting far from the fire pit in a darkened area at the foot of a large cottonwood tree.

We made our way over to them, where they sat with a group of kids on a pile of quilts and blankets, huddled close together for warmth. The entire group was made up of boy/girl couples. Even Anita had found a guy to sit with, a tall skinny kid with as many pimples as she had. At first, Beth did not see us. Then, after an awkward moment of standing at the edge of this clique, Laurie and I said, "Hi, Beth."

"Oh, hi," she said nonchalantly. "This is Danny." To him, she said, "These are the other friends I was telling you about."

Danny looked at Beth, smitten, then looked at us. He shrugged slightly and said, "Sorry, girls, no more room here."

Beth looked up at us smiling sweetly. "See you at breakfast." Then, she twiddled her woolly-gloved fingers in a wave. "Too-da-loo."

Laurie and I stepped back from them and looked at each other. Heads hanging, we trudged back to the fire pit to find seats, neither of us saying what was in our minds: Is this the Beth Peterson we thought we knew so well? Had we been "dismissed" so quickly after years of friendship?

Then, it was time for our guest speaker. A girl a little older than us stood up where everyone could see her. She was wearing new blue jeans, a white blouse and a navy sweater vest under her navy blue peacoat. Her hair was auburn and came past her shoulders, thick, straight and shiny. Everything about her was squeaky-clean.

"Hi, my name's Connie," she announced, "and tonight I'm going to tell you my own story about a lost sheep."

She waited for everyone to quiet down. "My story begins with Tammy, a girl who used to be my best friend. How many of you have a best friend? Raise your hand."

Over the quiet crackle of the campfire came the sound of rattling bracelets as various girls from our school raised their hands. At my school, best friends showed their loyalty by trading chain bracelets, which we called slave-bracelets or slave-chains. Some girls even got one from a Boy, if they were going steady. I looked at the one on my right wrist -—last year's birthday gift from Beth, a nice bracelet from a jewelry store, with a highly polished fat silver chain. It had an engraved name plate and a message etched on the back that said, "Nellie and Beth, BFF." I snuck a look at Laurie's wrist, and she had the kind of bracelet the poor kids wore, made from a length of dog chain from the local hardware store.

Connie continued, "I had a best friend all through grade school and we did everything together -—played Barbies, Twister, had slumber parties -—you name it! But when we started high school, things changed. My best friend Tammy started hanging around with new friends, people I didn't like very much. They ditched school, smoked cigarettes and some of the boys were loud and got in fistfights. I didn't know yet that our friendship was over."

It was hard to keep listening to Connie while I was watching Beth and Danny. He had his arms around her. When I looked at them, something didn't feel right. Was I jealous of Beth because she attracted a boyfriend and I didn't? Or was I hurt because for so many years we'd done everything together and now she hardly acknowledged me?

"-—a slumber party one night at one of the girls' houses. It was a night just like tonight, and the air was cold and dry. Tammy's mom drove us there and dropped us off. It was in a neighborhood I'd never been to before, even though it was in our school district. The girl's house was big, but it was also old and run down. They had wall-to-wall carpeting, but it had some tears in it, and the furniture was beat up. Then, I found out her parents weren't going to be home."

I looked over at Beth again and caught her and Danny in a slimy kiss. No, it wasn't jealousy I was feeling; it was something else. If Beth had to be with a boy, why couldn't it be someone nice, somebody I would like? Why did she pick a pot smoker who lived far away from us?

"-—the lights weren't very bright in this house, and it gave me a really creepy feeling. Then, one of the girls said that she wanted to have a séance and talk to dead people. Tammy thought this was a great idea, but I was scared. I wanted to go home. But how would I get out of there? My mom and dad were at the movies, so there was no way to reach them. Then I remembered that my Aunt Ruth lived nearby."

The fire was burning down. It was getting colder, so all of us began to feel the chill on our spines. We cupped our hands and blew hot breath into them to keep our noses from freezing off. As Connie continued talking, her voice got quieter and we had to strain to hear her.

"So, I pretended I had to go to the bathroom, but instead I snuck out the back door. As I walked down the gravel driveway, the crunch of my shoes was so loud I was sure someone would hear me and come out of the house to get me."

I saw Laurie looking in Beth's direction, so I looked, too, and we saw Beth and Danny and two other couples get up and leave the group. Laurie's expression reflected my thoughts, which can only be expressed as, "Uh-oh."

"-—and the car was moving slowly down the street toward me. I was so scared I didn't know whether to run and hide in some bushes or run back to the devil-house. The car's lights got closer, and it was slowing down—-"

Connie's voice was very low, now. "And when the car rolled to a stop beside me, the driver leaned across the seat and with a loud creak, the car door slowly swung open."

"Boo!" one of the boys yelled suddenly, and half of us screamed. Then, kids began to laugh and giggle nervously.

"It was Aunt Ruth!" Connie's voice became louder, now. "I was never so happy to see someone in my life! The car was warm and cozy inside and I shut the door quickly and locked it. 'Aunt Ruth, how did you know I was here?' I couldn't believe it!

"'Well,' she said, 'your mom called me a while ago to tell me you were spending the night in this neighborhood, but when she mentioned which house it was, I thought I'd better check on you. There have been some problems in the neighborhood from people living in that house."

The entire camp was quiet, now.

"I told her they wanted me to be in a séance, and she patted my hand. 'I have a better idea,' she said; 'warm cookies and milk, and then a bedtime story before you sleep over at my house.'

"I bet all of you know what bedtime story she told me," Connie said, looking across the sea of faces. We were too frozen to move. "It was the story from the Bible of the little lost lamb and the Shepherd who found it, and that night I was the lamb. Aunt Ruth and I stayed up for hours talking about God. In a few minutes, I will be walking around with the teachers to answer any questions you may have."

* * *

Usually, I'm a sound sleeper because of years of living in a clapboard farmhouse where Poppa and my brothers had to get up early to feed the cattle and collect eggs. That night, I'm not sure I even went to sleep. First, there was the warm feeling in my heart after hearing Connie's story. But at the same time, I felt a growing sense of concern because Beth was not back yet. I knew she was with Danny, but I couldn't understand why none of the teachers realized she was missing. And I was also wondering what she and Danny were doing in the middle of the night. I already knew what she would say in the morning: "We were just talking."

It seemed like forever, but finally I heard the door to our sleeping-room creak open and a soft giggle, then "Too-da-loo." It was Beth, and I wanted to jump up and run to her, to tell her I'd been worried, but something held me back as I made slit-eyes to watch her pick her way among the sleeping campers, stumbling and giggling. A sweet smell trailed after her and I closed my eyes completely and sighed. That sweet smell had been described to me before, so I had an idea what it was: marijuana.

In the morning, I was one of the first ones to wake up. It was almost seven, which is very late for a ranch girl. A swinging door in our sleeping-room had been opened onto a large kitchen, where the sound of bacon frying and the smell of coffee for the grown-ups filled the air. I glanced over at Beth, still sleeping, her mouth half open and a light snore coming out. Several of the girls were looking at her, pointing and giggling. I noticed the brownish red stains in her blonde hair and on her cheeks. When she'd come in last night, she'd forgotten that her sweater was on top of her pillow, and she'd laid her head in the sloppy joe sauce. Embarrassed for her, I looked away.

Beth and Anita didn't sit with us at breakfast. Laurie and I joined some of the girls we'd met last night, and in the back of my mind I remembered what Connie had said about her own best friend, Tammy -—that a time came when she knew their friendship was over. I wondered if this was going to happen between Beth and me, as I looked across the room and saw her teasing Danny. Yet, I found I was not completely unhappy with the girls I was eating with. Afterward, we returned to our sleeping-room so we could begin packing our bags to take the bus home. Laurie and I boarded with Mrs. Casaverde, who was now directing a game of Alphabet. The bus engine started. Its fumes filtered in through an open window.

Laurie pulled on my sleeve. "Isn't that Beth over there, by the church door?"

I looked.

"She's going to miss the bus," Laurie worried.

"Oh, I don't think so," I said, "they'll wait for her."

The bus shifted gears and rolled forward slightly its front door slamming shut.

"Wait!" Laurie and I cried out together, but the Alphabet Game just got louder as we looked at each other in fear.

We continued to watch as Beth dawdled with Danny, unconcerned that she was losing her ride.

"I guess her parents will have to come pick her up," I said.

"'G!'" Laurie called out.

"Where?" someone challenged.

* * *

We arrived home late Saturday morning and I was quiet when my big brother Jim picked me up in our church parking lot. I was glad he'd come instead of Momma, because he was in college now so he was too old and too sophisticated to make small talk with his frosh sister. He was still the same thin-faced, dark-haired guy I'd grown up with, only now he shaved and drove a car. I didn't mind that he didn't talk much; I had a lot to think about.

And I was still thinking on Sunday morning as I sat near the front of our church with my family. My wrist felt naked without the slave-bracelet Beth had given me. I'd taken it off when I got home from Teen Winter Camp.

Our church was beautifully decorated for Christmas, and on the platform behind the choir was a twelve-foot-high fake tree with white flocking. It had been dressed up with silky red poinsettias, shiny gold balls, and red and white twinkle lights. Laurie leaned over to whisper in my ear, "Notice something really cool about that tree?"

I shook my head "no."

She explained: "If you look between the branches, the stained glass window shows through like extra ornaments. Isn't it pretty?"

She was right. It was very pretty.

The minister opened his Bible to 1 Peter 2:25 and asked us to read aloud with him: "For ye are as sheep going astray; but are now returned unto the Shepherd and Bishop of your souls."

"Did you hear what happened to Beth?" Laurie asked. I nodded, but she said it anyway. "Grounded for a month. But I heard she's already planning how to sneak out to see Danny."

I shook my head slowly back and forth and so did Laurie.

Sometimes a bad decision doesn't seem that wrong at the time, but the next one is worse. It didn't look like these bad decisions of hers were going to stop any time soon, and since I'd been taught that one bad decision could lead to another, I wondered how Beth would end up.

Acknowledgments:

Thank you to those who critiqued me as I developed my work: Coffee House Writers' Group; The Ninos; St. John's (Covina); and Northkirk Writers' Group.

Also by this author:

The One Percent Cat
> (ANIMALS IN MYSTERIES VOLUME 1 anthology, Fall 2023)
> *'Only one percent of lost pets make it back to their original owners...'*
> *This is the story of a one percent cat.*

One Night at Fred's
> (TROUBLE IN TUCSON anthology, Feb. 2023)
> *"Love is something that can't be explained by anyone besides the one who feels it."*

Darker
> (ROCK AND A HARD PLACE Magazine, Feb. 2023)
> *"Under different circumstances, we might be compatible."*

Everything
> (SoWest LOVE KILLS anthology, August 2021)
> *When asked if I was looking for anything in particular, I said, "I'll know it when I see it."*

Please follow Elena E. Smith in her author Facebook group, MAHUENGA

About the Author

Elena E. Smith is a hard-boiled cozy writer who grew up in Arizona then spent her adult life in Los Angeles. She has had four separate careers (with some overlap, of course - she's not a hundred years old), including entry-level jobs in the entertainment industry, advertising sales account executive, paralegal, and mobile home sales. She has been to London and Paris, owned her own horse, and enjoyed playing guitar and singing. She has a Bachelor's degree in Adult Basic Education (CSULB) and an AA in Criminal Justice. She is now retired and spends her time writing and hanging out with her husband, her cat and her friends. Smith has had a number of short stories published and will soon release her first novel, MAHUENGA, about a former cop/ recovering alcoholic who's looking for a missing teenage girl.